W9-BUP-966

PENGUIN BOOKS

AVOCADO IS NOT YOUR COLOR
AND OTHER SCENES OF
MARRIED BLISS

Edward Frascino is a bachelor. Born in the Bronx, near the zoo, he grew up on comic strips and movies. He's been here and there, done this and that, and lives in Manhattan, where he draws cartoons for *The New Yorker*. Mr. Frascino likes cats.

Avocado Is

and Other Scenes

Cartoons by

Not Your Color
of Married Bliss

Edward Frascino

PENGUIN BOOKS

Penguin Books Ltd, Harmondsworth,
Middlesex, England
Penguin Books, 625 Madison Avenue,
New York, New York 10022, U.S.A.
Penguin Books Australia Ltd, Ringwood,
Victoria, Australia
Penguin Books Canada Limited, 2801 John Street,
Markham, Ontario, Canada L3R 1B4
Penguin Books (N.Z.) Ltd, 182–190 Wairau Road,
Auckland 10, New Zealand

First published 1983

LIBRARY OF CONGRESS CATALOGING IN PUBLICATION DATA
Frascino, Edward.
Avocado is not your color and other scenes of
married bliss.
1. Marriage—Caricatures and cartoons.
2. American wit and humor, Pictorial.   I. Title.
NC1429.F6676A4   1983   741.5'973   82-16153
ISBN 0 14 00.6364 1

Printed in the United States of America by
R. R. Donnelley & Sons Company, Harrisonburg, Virginia

Of the 106 cartoons in this book, 105 originally
appeared in *The New Yorker* and were copyrighted ©
in the years 1969 through 1982, inclusive, by
The New Yorker Magazine, Inc.

"Something for your sweet tooth."

"Quick! Your gut reaction."

"Avocado is not your color."

"I'm trying to think of the word in French."

"Can you show us something else? This one makes him look too old."

"For heaven's sake! When did you have your ear pierced?"

"You're sure this doesn't look funny without a tan?"

"Too sexy."

"*I married her because she laughed like Ginger Rogers.*"

*"The girl I fell in love with and married was an airline stewardess.
An airline stewardess, Marie! Have you forgotten
what that once meant to you?"*

"My husband says, 'No surprises.'"

"I think I liked you better as a blonde."

"*I'm thinking of changing my perfume. Unless, of course, you are particularly fond of this one.*"

"I wish I could ad-lib."

"Why don't <u>we</u> have a battle of wits sometime?"

"It's a variety show. There's something in it for everyone."

"It appears I'm the only one with a built-in immunity
to your infectious laugh."

"*Did you hear that laugh a split second ahead of all the others?*
That was Howard."

"*Excuse me, sir. May I see your ticket stubs, please?*"

"And this is the little woman — a person in her own right."

"Preston, <u>must</u> you bid in your Donald Duck voice?"

"*Do you know the Kendalls? They, too, are inseparable.*"

"*Everything was truly great, sir. How did we do?*"

"Nothing you say is ever passed around the dinner table."

"My face hurts from too much laughing."

"The checkout girl just got back from two weeks in Portugal, Spain, and Morocco. And <u>we're</u> spending eight days in Cape May."

"*Very charming, but you promised this year we'd ride a raft down the Colorado River.*"

"For heaven's sake, Sheldon, put on your glasses."

"Come and meet Sandra, dear. Sandra is one of those
lucky blondes with easy-to-tan skin."

"No, I don't want to know where you've got it hidden.
I'm jittery enough just knowing you've got it."

"Come on, Harve. Do your Quasimodo for us."

"We can't be lost. This is the only damn highway
they've got up here."

"Damn it all! We're out of gas!"

"With the fare increase and all, how much does a hot time in the old town cost us now?"

"I've been wondering, Delphine. Do the poor still get poorer?"

"But I don't understand, Foster. I thought you said
we could laugh at inflation."

"Not the easiest man in the kingdom to live with, needless to say, but a damned good provider."

"*I guess they really mean it. Here's a <u>second</u> appeal for
funds from Brad and Dee Dee Dennison.*"

"I saw Grace Dworthman, Alice Parsons, and Mildred Livingston
today. They all send you their love."

"There's something I've been meaning to discuss with you, Miriam.
Roy Gillis asked me what our scene was,
and I didn't know what to answer."

"I added ginger to wake up the peas."

"I remember opening the can, and I remember washing the pot,
but I don't remember eating the chili."

"*Was I dreaming, or did you waken me with a kiss?*"

"I feel lucky today."

"I had that awful dream again. I was the President of the
United States and the Marine Corps Band refused to
play 'Hail to the Chief.'"

"Election Day is dawning, and I'm still undecided."

"I know the doctor said this is only a bad cold, but in case he's mistaken I'd like to hear side eight of 'Der Rosenkavalier' one last time."

"Remember when you had the flu two years ago and you started 'Remembrance of Things Past'? Do you want to try finishing it now?"

"Why don't you go out and sit under your tree?"

"I didn't go back to work after lunch. I got homesick."

"What do you consider your biggest fault, and what
are you going to do about it?"

"When people ask what you're like, I say you're a saint.
That usually shuts them up."

"If not with me, just where do your sympathies lie?"

"Yes, I have to admit you've always been nice to me,
but you're nice to everyone."

"You're always telling me you know exactly how I feel.
Well, this time I'm calling your bluff.
Exactly how <u>do</u> I feel?"

"You _are_ happy. But, like everything else, you keep it bottled up inside."

"Everything reminds me of you."

"Don't be silly. If you were afflicted with a multiple
personality, I'd have noticed something."

"You've proved to me beyond a shadow of a doubt that
truth is stranger than fiction."

"You leave nothing to the imagination."

"To you, my dear. In twenty-seven years you've never stepped out of character."

"I guess ours is the old story—too much of a good thing."

"You must admit we've never wanted for coziness."

"We're just a couple of homebodies."

*"I'll be right back. I'm going to telephone for
the correct time."*

"*Heather and Mel Spelcher want us to come over just for the fun of it.*"

"Tell me, Elliot, have we ever done anything just for the hell of it?"

"They say touch dancing is coming back."

"Don't you know some place with a mechanical bull?"

"Madeline plays strictly for her own amusement."

"*Now do you see what I mean when I say I've had the role of aggressor forced upon me?*"

"I wish you could agree with me without gritting your teeth."

"Raymond! Stop being evasive!"

"*First of all, is this new anger or merely some old anger you're just getting around to expressing?*"

"I happen to be a very useful man to know."

"I love it when you call me Mr. Know-It-All."

"What do you say we throw in the towel and say good night?"

"*Thus ends civilization as you have known it.*"

"*Don't tell me. You've left Roy. Your brother arrived this morning. He's left Joyce. It's going to be an old-fashioned Christmas after all.*"

*"When you're suffocating, it's unimportant why you're suffocating.
It's only important to get air."*

"Adios, Ned."

"Howard, this is one of the toughest decisions
I've ever had to make."

"To make a long story short, good-bye."

"I'll kiss, but I won't make up."

"Honey, blow me a kiss."

"Morris, do you ever have erotic fantasies?"

"The night, they say, was made for love."

"Well, Alfred, the children have grown up, got married, and left home.
Do you still want me to run away with you?"

"Oh, that's Mignon. She's the magic ingredient in our marriage."

"He knows I can't stand it when he doesn't eat."

"Trudy."

"You wouldn't have lasted five minutes with Henry the Eighth."

"Come on, now. It's my turn to hold the scepter."

"Go away! I'm a happily married woman."

"I didn't always have this mustache, and if I'm not mistaken,
you used to be a blonde. Weren't we married to each other
from 1952 through 1956?"

"Samantha is Harry's, but Homer here is mine
from a previous marriage."

"My first husband didn't smoke, either, but he always carried matches to light mine."

"Do you remember this darling thing I found in the attic?
Is it mine by my second husband or yours
by your third wife?"

*"When Grandma met Grandpa, he was already married,
but to a woman who didn't understand him."*

"*Tell me, Edgar, did you, at any of those times you went out for a loaf of bread, ever toy with the idea of never coming back?*"

*"Lucy Mae, did you ever sit under the apple tree
with anyone else but me?"*

"Remember that joke I always laughed at so hard? The one you
used to tell about the horse with the wooden leg?
I don't get it."

"Well, here we are in the shade of the old apple tree, down by the
old millstream. We've come here on a bicycle built for two.
You're wearing a tulip, and I'm wearing a big, red rose.
But have we recaptured that old magic?"

"There's a side of me you haven't seen yet."